ROBERT LOUIS STEVENSON'S

Treasure Island

THE GRAPHIC NOVEL

adapted by
Tim Hamilton

PUFFIN BOOKS

Visit us at www.abdopub.com

Spotlight, a division of ABDO Publishing Company, is a distributor of high quality reinforced library bound editions for schools and libraries.

This library bound edition is published by arrangement with Penguin Young Readers Group, a member of Penguin Group (USA) Inc.

Library of Congress Cataloging-In-Publication Data

PUFFIN BOOKS
Published by the Penguin Group
Penguin Young Readers Group,
345 Hudson Street, New York, NY 10014 U.S.A.

Treasure Island Graphic Novel first published by Puffin Books, a division of Penguin Young Readers Group, 2005

A Byron Preiss Book
Byron Preiss Visual Publications
24 West 25th Street, New York, NY 10010

Adapted by Tim Hamilton
Cover art by Tim Hamilton
Series Editor: Dwight Jon Zimmerman
Series Assistant Editor: April Isaacs
Interior design by Matt Postawa, Raul Carvajal and Gilda Hannah
Cover design by Matt Postawa

Puffin Books ISBN 0-14-240470-5
ISBN: 1-59961-119-8 Reinforced Library Bound Edition

ROBERT LOUIS STEVENSON'S

Treasure Island

SQUIRE TRELAWNEY, DR. LIVESEY, AND THE REST OF THE *GENTLEMEN* HAVING ASKED ME TO WRITE DOWN THE PARTICULARS ABOUT *TREASURE ISLAND*, FROM BEGINNING TO END, I TAKE UP THE *PEN...*

...AND GO BACK TO THE TIME WHEN MY FATHER KEPT THE *ADMIRAL BENBOW INN*, AND THE BROWN OLD *SEAMAN*, WITH THE SABER CUT, FIRST TOOK UP LODGINGS UNDER OUR ROOF.

I *REMEMBER* HIM AS IF IT WAS YESTERDAY...

WHEN *MY FATHER* APPEARED, HE CALLED ROUGHLY FOR A GLASS OF RUM.

THIS IS A *HANDY COVE*, AND A PLEASANT SITTYATED GROG-SHOP. MUCH *COMPANY*, MATE?

MY FATHER TOLD HIM NO.

THEN THIS IS THE *BERTH* FOR ME.

HE WAS A VERY *SILENT MAN* BY CUSTOM

EVERY DAY, WHEN HE CAME BACK FROM HIS *STROLL*, HE WOULD ASK IF ANY SEAFARING *MEN* HAD GONE BY ALONG THE ROAD.

AT FIRST WE THOUGHT IT WAS THE WANT OF *COMPANY* OF HIS OWN KIND THAT MADE HIM ASK THIS QUESTION.

BUT WE BEGAN TO SEE HE WAS DESIROUS TO *AVOID* THEM.

WHEN A SEAMAN PUT UP AT THE *ADMIRAL BENBOW*, HE WAS ALWAYS SURE TO BE AS *SILENT* AS A MOUSE WHEN ANY SUCH WAS *PRESENT*.

FOR ME, AT LEAST, THERE WAS NO *SECRET* ABOUT THE MATTER; FOR I WAS, IN A WAY, A *SHARER* IN HIS *ALARMS*.

HE HAD PROMISED ME A *SILVER FOURPENNY* ON THE FIRST OF EVERY MONTH IF I WOULD ONLY KEEP MY "WEATHER-EYE OPEN FOR A *SEAFARING MAN* WITH ONE LEG."

AND LET HIM KNOW THE *MOMENT* HE APPEARED.

"THE SEAFARING MAN WITH ONE *LEG*."

HOW THAT PERSONAGE HAUNTED *MY DREAMS*, I NEED SCARCELY TELL YOU.

ON STORMY NIGHTS, I WOULD SEE HIM IN A *THOUSAND FORMS*.

AND WITH A THOUSAND *DIABOLICAL EXPRESSIONS*.

TO SEE HIM *PURSUE* ME OVER HEDGE AND DITCH WAS THE WORST OF *NIGHTMARES.*

I PAID *PRETTY DEAR* FOR MY MONTHLY FOURPENNY PIECE, IN THE SHAPE OF THESE *ABOMINABLE FANCIES.*

BUT THOUGH I WAS SO TERRIFIED BY THE IDEA OF THE SEAFARING MAN WITH ONE *LEG...*

I WAS FAR *LESS AFRAID* OF THE *CAPTAIN* HIMSELF THAN ANYBODY ELSE WHO *KNEW* HIM.

HIS *STORIES* WERE WHAT FRIGHTENED PEOPLE MOST OF ALL. MY *FATHER* WAS ALWAYS SAYING THE INN WOULD BE *RUINED.*

PEOPLE WERE *FRIGHTENED* AT THE TIME, BUT ON LOOKING BACK, THEY RATHER *LIKED* IT; IT WAS A FINE *EXCITEMENT* IN A QUIET COUNTRY LIFE.

HE WAS ONLY ONCE *CROSSED*, AND THAT WAS TOWARDS THE *END.*

WHEN MY POOR *FATHER* WAS FAR GONE IN A *DECLINE.*

DR. *LIVESEY* CAME LATE ONE AFTERNOON TO SEE THE *PATIENT,* THEN WENT INTO THE *PARLOR.*

SUDDENLY, THE *CAPTAIN* BEGAN TO PIPE UP HIS ETERNAL *SONG.*

YO HO HO

AND A BOTTLE OF RUM

DR. LIVESEY WAS TALKING TO OLD TAYLOR, THE GARDENER, ON A NEW CURE FOR THE RHEUMATICS WHEN...

SILENCE THERE BETWEEN DECKS!

IF YOU KEEP ON DRINKING RUM, THE WORLD WILL SOON BE QUIT OF A VERY DIRTY SCOUNDREL.

THE CAPTAIN SPRANG TO HIS FEET... OPENED A SAILOR'S CLASP-KNIFE, AND THREATENED TO PIN THE DOCTOR TO THE WALL.

IF YOU DO NOT PUT THAT KNIFE *DOWN*, I PROMISE UPON MY HONOR, YOU WILL *HANG*.

I'M NOT A DOCTOR ONLY, I'M A *MAGISTRATE*. IF I CATCH A BREATH OF *COMPLAINT* AGAINST YOU, I'LL HAVE YOU *HUNTED DOWN*.

FIFTEEN MEN ON...

IT WAS NOT VERY LONG AFTER THIS THAT THERE OCCURRED THE FIRST OF THE *MYSTERIOUS EVENTS* THAT RID US OF THE CAPTAIN, THOUGH NOT OF HIS AFFAIRS.

WINTER ARRIVED BITTER COLD, AND MY POOR *FATHER* SEEMED UNLIKELY TO SEE SPRING AS HE FELL MORE INTO *ILLNESS.*

THEN, ONE JANUARY MORNING...

IS THIS HERE TABLE FOR MY MATE, *BILL?*

I TOLD HIM I DID NOT *KNOW* HIS MATE BILL.

THIS WAS FOR A PERSON WHOM WE CALLED THE *CAPTAIN*.

WELL, MY MATE BILL WOULD BE CALLED THE *CAPTAIN*, AS LIKE AS NOT.

NOW, IS MY MATE *BILL* IN THIS HERE HOUSE?

I TOLD HIM HE WAS OUT WALKING.

AH, THIS'LL BE AS GOOD AS *DRINK* TO MY MATE BILL.

"WE'LL GIVE BILL A LITTLE *SURPRISE*, BLESS HIS 'ART."

19

FOR A LONG TIME, I COULD HEAR *NOTHING* BUT A LOW GABBLING. THEN...

NO, NO, NO, *NO*; AND AN *END* OF IT!

IF IT COMES TO SWINGING *SWING ALL* SAY I.

THEN ALL OF A SUDDEN THERE WAS A TREMENDOUS *EXPLOSION* OF OATHS AND OTHER NOISES.

I SAW BLACK DOG IN FULL *FLIGHT*, AND THE CAPTAIN HOTLY *PURSUING.*

THUNK!

JIM...!

ARE YOU *HURT?*

RUM...!

22

IT WAS A HAPPY *RELIEF* FOR US WHEN DOCTOR LIVESEY CAME IN, ON A *VISIT* TO MY FATHER.

OH, DOCTOR. WHERE IS HE *WOUNDED?*

WOUNDED? A FIDDLE-STICK'S END! THE MAN HAS HAD A *STROKE.*

WHERE'S BLACK DOG?

THERE IS NO BLACK DOG HERE. NOW, MR. *BONES...*

THAT'S NOT MY *NAME.*

MUCH I *CARE.*

NOW MIND YOU, I CLEAR MY *CONSCIENCE...* THE NAME OF RUM FOR YOU IS *DEATH.*

LATER THAT DAY, AT ABOUT NOON...

JIM, *HOW LONG* DID THAT DOCTOR SAY I HAD TO LIE IN THIS *BERTH?*

A *WEEK* AT LEAST.

A *WEEK!* I CAN'T *DO* THAT. THEY'D HAVE THE *BLACKSPOT* ON ME BY THEN.

JIM, YOU SAW THAT *SEAFARING MAN* TODAY?

BLACK DOG?

HE'S A *BAD ONE.* BUT THERE'S *WORSE* THAN PUT HIM ON.

MIND YOU, IT'S MY *SEA CHEST* THEY'RE AFTER.

I WAS *OLD FLINT'S FIRST MATE,* AND I'M THE ONLY ONE AS KNOWS THE *PLACE.* HE GAVE IT ME WHEN HE LAY *A-DYING,* LIKE AS IF I WAS TO NOW.

BUT YOU WON'T PEACH UNLESS THEY GET THE *BLACK SPOT* ON ME.

OR UNLESS YOU SEE THAT BLACK DOG AGAIN, OR A SEAFARING MAN WITH *ONE LEG,* JIM...HIM ABOVE ALL.

BUT WHAT IS THE *BLACK SPOT,* CAPTAIN?

THAT'S A *SUMMONS,* MATE. I'LL TELL YOU IF THEY GET THAT.

BUT KEEP YOUR WEATHER-EYE *OPEN,* JIM, AND I'LL SHARE WITH YOU *EQUALS,* UPON MY HONOUR.

PROBABLY I SHOULD HAVE *TOLD* THE WHOLE *STORY* TO THE DOCTOR. BUT AS THINGS FELL OUT, MY POOR FATHER *DIED* QUITE SUDDENLY THAT EVENING.

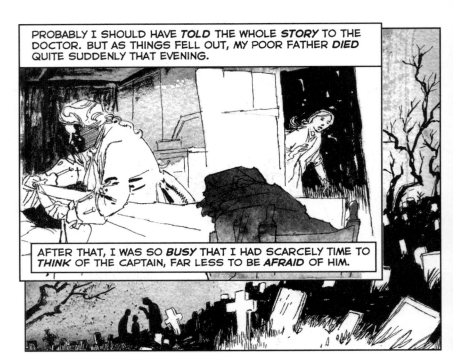

AFTER THAT, I WAS SO *BUSY* THAT I HAD SCARCELY TIME TO *THINK* OF THE CAPTAIN, FAR LESS TO BE *AFRAID* OF HIM.

THE CAPTAIN HAD AN ALARMING WAY NOW...OF DRAWING HIS CUTLASS AND LAYING IT BARE BEFORE HIM.

BUT, HE MINDED PEOPLE LESS, AND SEEMED SHUT UP IN HIS OWN THOUGHTS.

SO THINGS PASSED UNTIL, THE DAY AFTER THE FUNERAL...

TAP
TAP
TAP

TAP
TAP
TAP

TAP
TAP
TAP

WILL ANY KIND FRIEND INFORM A *POOR BLIND MAN,* WHO HAS LOST HIS SIGHT IN THE SERVICE OF *ENGLAND,* WHERE OR IN WHAT PART OF THE COUNTRY HE MAY NOW BE?

TAP
TAP
TAP

YOU AREA AT THE ADMIRAL BENBOW, BLACK HILL COVE, MY GOOD MAN.

WILL YOU GIVE ME YOUR *HAND,* MY KIND YOUNG FRIEND, AND LEAD ME IN?

CREAK

HERE'S A *FRIEND* FOR YOU, BILL.

NOW, BILL, SIT WHERE YOU ARE. IF I CAN'T SEE, I CAN *HEAR* A FINGER STIRRING.

BUSINESS IS *BUSINESS.*

HOLD OUT YOUR *LEFT HAND.* BOY, TAKE HIS LEFT HAND BY THE *WRIST,* AND BRING IT NEAR TO *MY RIGHT.*

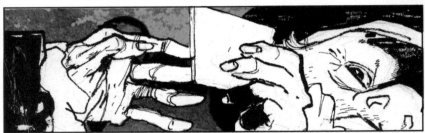

AND NOW
THAT'S *DONE!*

TAP
TAP
TAP
TAP

TEN O'CLOCK! GIVES US *SIX HOURS.* WE'LL DO THEM *YET.*

SUDDENLY, HE *REELED,* PUT HIS HAND TO HIS *THROAT,* AND THEN *FELL.*

ADMIRAL BENBOW

THE CAPTAIN HAD BEEN STRUCK *DEAD* BY THUNDERING *APOPLEXY.*

TAP
TAP
TAP

31

I LOST NO TIME IN TELLING MY MOTHER ALL THAT I KNEW. WE SAW OURSELVES AT ONCE IN A DIFFICULT AND DANGEROUS POSITION.

IT SEEMED IMPOSSIBLE FOR EITHER OF US TO REMAIN MUCH LONGER IN THE *HOUSE.* IT OCCURRED TO US TO GO FORTH TOGETHER AND SEEK HELP IN THE NEIGHBORING HAMLET.

WHAT GREATLY ENCOURAGED ME WAS THAT IT WAS IN AN *OPPOSITE DIRECTION* FROM THAT WHENCE THE BLIND MAN HAD MADE HIS APPEARANCE.

IT WAS ALREADY *CANDLE-LIGHT* WHEN WE REACHED THE HAMLET.

BUT NO SOUL WOULD CONSENT TO *RETURN* WITH US TO THE ADMIRAL BENBOW. THE MORE WE TOLD OF OUR *TROUBLES*, THE MORE, MAN, WOMAN, AND CHILD, THEY CLUNG TO THE SHELTER OF THEIR HOUSES.

THE NAME OF *CAPTAIN FLINT*, THOUGH IT WAS STRANGE TO ME, WAS WELL ENOUGH KNOWN TO SOME THERE, AND CARRIED A GREAT WEIGHT OF TERROR.

WHILE WE COULD GET *SEVERAL* WHO WERE WILLING ENOUGH TO RIDE TO DR. LIVESEY'S...

...WHICH LAY IN ANOTHER DIRECTION, NONE WOULD *HELP* US TO DEFEND THE INN.

33

ALL THEY WOULD DO WAS TO GIVE ME A *LOADED PISTOL,* AND TO PROMISE TO HAVE *HORSES* READY SADDLED, IN CASE WE WERE *PURSUED.*

MY *HEART* WAS BEATING FINELY WHEN WE TWO SET FORTH *BACK* TO THE ADMIRAL BENBOW.

WE HAVE TO GET THE *KEY* OFF THAT!

PERHAPS IT'S ROUND HIS *NECK.*

AFTER WE FOUND THE KEY, WE HURRIED *UPSTAIRS.*

GIVE ME THE *KEY.*

TAP TAP TAP TAP TAP TAP TAP TAP TAP TAP

TAP TAP TAP TAP TAP TAP TAP TAP TAP TAP

TAP TAP TAP TAP TAP TAP TAP TAP TAP TAP

ROUT THE HOUSE OUT. THEY MUST BE *CLOSE!*

BUT, JUST AS THEY BEGAN *SEARCHING...*

K-POW

THE *BUCCANEERS* TURNED AT ONCE AND *RAN.*

JOHNNY, BLACK DOG, DIRK! YOU WON'T *LEAVE* OLD PEW, MATES!

I LEAPED TO MY FEET AND *HAILED* THE RIDERS. THEY WERE *REVENUE OFFICERS* AND TO THEM MY MOTHER AND I OWED OUR *PRESERVATION* FROM DEATH.

PEW WAS DEAD, *STONE DEAD.* BUT HIS MATES MADE IT TO THEIR *LUGGER* IN KIT'S HOLE AND *ESCAPED.* REVENUE SUPERVISOR DANCE SAID HE STOOD "LIKE A FISH OUT OF WATER" AS HE WATCHED THE SHIP DISAPPEAR.

THEY GOT OFF *CLEAN,* AND THERE'S AN END.

I WENT WITH MR. DANCE *BACK* TO THE ADMIRAL BENBOW.

YOU CANNOT *IMAGINE* A HOUSE IN SUCH A STATE OF SMASH.

WELL, THEN, HAWKINS, WHAT IN *FORTUNE* WERE THEY AFTER?

I BELIEVE I HAVE THE *THING* IN MY BREAST POCKET.

I SHOULD LIKE TO GET IT PUT IN *SAFETY.*

I THOUGHT, PERHAPS, *DR. LIVESEY...*

PERFECTLY *RIGHT.* A GENTLEMAN AND A *MAGISTRATE.*

"I MIGHT AS WELL *ROUND THERE* MYSELF," HE SAID. "HAWKINS, I'LL TAKE YOU ALONG. DOGGER, YOU HAVE A GOOD HORSE, TAKE UP THIS LAD *BEHIND* YOU."

WE FOUND DR. LIVESEY AT THE HOME OF *SQUIRE TRELAWNEY.*

IT WAS THERE THAT WE *TOLD* WHAT HAD OCCURRED. I GAVE DR. LIVESEY THE CAPTAIN'S *OILSKIN PACKET.*

"YOU HAVE *HEARD* OF THIS *FLINT,* SQUIRE?" ASKED DR. LIVESEY.

HE WAS THE *BLOODTHIRSTIEST* BUCCANEER THAT SAILED.

HMMMM. "BULK OF TREASURE *HERE.*"

LIVESEY, IN THREE WEEK'S TIME, WE'LL HAVE THE *BEST SHIP* IN SEARCH OF THAT SPOT.

WE'LL HAVE *MONEY* TO *ROLL IN...* TO PLAY DUCKS AND DRAKES WITH EVER AFTER, LIVESEY!

WE ARE NOT THE *ONLY MEN* WHO KNOW OF THIS *PAPER.* THESE FELLOWS WHO ATTACKED THE INN TONIGHT....

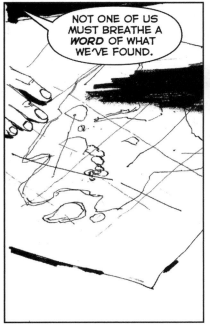

NOT ONE OF US MUST BREATHE A *WORD* OF WHAT WE'VE FOUND.

LIVESEY, YOU ARE ALWAYS IN THE *RIGHT* OF IT. I'LL BE AS *SILENT* AS THE GRAVE.

IT WAS LONGER THAN THE SQUIRE IMAGINED ERE WE WERE *READY* FOR THE SEA. I RECEIVED A *LETTER* DATED MARCH 1, FROM SQUIRE TRELAWNEY.

"THE *SHIP* IS BOUGHT AND FITTED. SHE LIES AT ANCHOR, READY FOR SEA. NAME: *HISPANIOLA*.

"WITH THE *CREW*, I HAD THE MOST REMARKABLE STROKE OF FORTUNE. *LONG JOHN SILVER*, WHO LOST A LEG IN HIS COUNTRY'S SERVICE, I ENGAGED AS A *COOK*. THANKS TO HIM, I NOW HAVE A *CREW*.

"COME FULL SPEED TO *BRISTOL*."

I SAID *GOODBYE* TO MOTHER AND THE ADMIRAL BENBOW, AND A FEW DAYS *LATER* I ARRIVED IN BRISTOL.

JIM, HERE YOU ARE!

THE DOCTOR CAME LAST NIGHT. *BRAVO!* THE SHIP'S COMPANY *COMPLETE!*

OH, SIR, *WHEN* DO WE *SAIL?*

SAIL! WE SAIL *TOMORROW!*

I SEE. YOU ARE OUR NEW *CABIN BOY.* PLEASE I AM TO SEE YOU.

MR. SILVER, SIR?

YES, MY LAD, SUCH IS MY *NAME*, TO BE SURE.

WELL, SQUIRE, I DON'T PUT MUCH *FAITH* IN YOUR *DISCOVERIES*, AS A GENERAL THING.

BUT I WILL SAY THIS, JOHN SILVER *SUITS* ME.

THE MAN'S A PERFECT *TRUMP*.

AND NOW, JIM MAY COME *ON BOARD* WITH US, MAY HE NOT?

TO BE SURE HE *MAY.*

TAKE YOUR *HAT,* HAWKINS, AND WE'LL *SEE* THE SHIP.

THE *HISPANIOLA* LAY SOME WAY OUT, AND WE WENT UNDER THE *FIGUREHEADS* AND ROUND THE STERNS OF MANY OTHER SHIPS.

AT LAST, HOWEVER WE GOT *ALONGSIDE.* I SOON OBSERVED THAT THINGS WERE *NOT FRIENDLY* BETWEEN MR. TRELAWNEY AND THE CAPTAIN.

WELL, *CAPTAIN SMOLLETT,* ALL WELL, I HOPE. ALL *SHIPSHAPE* AND SEAWORTHY?

WELL, SIR, BETTER SPEAK *PLAIN.*

I *DON'T LIKE* THIS CRUISE. I DON'T LIKE THE *MEN.* AND I DON'T LIKE MY OFFICER.

I WAS ENGAGED, SIR, ON WHAT WE CALL *SEALED ORDERS.*

BUT NOW I FIND THAT *EVERY MAN* BEFORE THE MAST *KNOWS MORE* THAN I DO.

NEXT, I LEARN WE ARE GOING AFTER *TREASURE.* I DON'T LIKE TREASURE VOYAGES. AND I DON'T LIKE THEM, ABOVE ALL, WHEN THEY ARE *SECRET.*

THE CREW. ARE THEY NOT *GOOD SEAMEN?*

I THINK I SHOULD HAVE HAD THE *CHOOSING* OF MY OWN HANDS.

HEAR ME A FEW WORDS *MORE!* THERE'S BEEN TOO MUCH *BLABBIN'!*

FAR TOO MUCH.

I AM *RESPONSIBLE* FOR THE SHIP'S *SAFETY.*

I ASK YOU TO TAKE CERTAIN *PRECAUTIONS.* AND YOU'LL FIND I DO MY *DUTY.*

A LITTLE BEFORE *DAWN,* THE BOATSWAIN SOUNDED HIS *PIPE,* AND THE CREW BEGAN TO MAN THE *CAPSTAINS.*

ALL WAS SO *NEW* AND INTERESTING TO ME... THE BRIEF *COMMANDS,* THE SHRILL NOTE OF THE *WHISTLE,* THE MEN BUSTLING TO THEIR PLACES IN THE *GLIMMER* OF THE SHIP'S LANTERNS.

FIFTEEN MEN ON THE *DEAD MAN'S* CHEST...

YO-HO-HO, AND A BOTTLE OF RUM!

I AM NOT GOING TO RELATE THAT *VOYAGE* IN DETAIL.

THE SHIP PROVED TO BE A *GOOD SHIP.*

THE CREW WERE *CAPABLE SEAMEN.*

AND THE CAPTAIN THOROUGHLY *UNDERSTOOD* HIS BUSINESS.

BUT THE *ONE MAN* ALL THE CREW RESPECTED AND EVEN *OBEYED* WAS *LONG JOHN SILVER.*

TO ME HE WAS UNWEARIEDLY *KIND;* AND ALWAYS GLAD TO SEE ME IN THE *GALLEY.*

COME, HAWKINS, COME AND HAVE A *YARN* WITH JOHN. NOBODY MORE *WELCOME* THAN YOURSELF, MY SON.

HERE'S *CAP'N FLINT...* I CALLS MY PARROT CAP'N FLINT, AFTER THE FAMOUS *BUCCANEER.*

NOW, THAT BIRD IS, MAYBE, *TWO HUNDRED* YEARS OLD, HAWKINS.

AND IF ANYBODY'S SEEN MORE *WICKEDNESS,* IT MUST BE THE *DEVIL* HIMSELF.

STAND BY TO GO ABOUT!

HE WOULD GIVE HER *SUGAR* FROM HIS POCKET, AND THEN THE BIRD WOULD *SWEAR* STRAIGHT ON.

THERE, YOU CAN'T TOUCH *PITCH* AND NOT BE *MUCKED*, LAD.

HERE'S THIS POOR OL' *INNOCENT BIRD* O' MINE SWEARING BLUE FIRE, AND NONE THE *WISER*, YOU MAY LAY TO THAT.

AND JOHN WOULD TOUCH HIS FORELOCK WITH A *SOLEMN WAY* HE HAD, THAT MADE ME THINK HE WAS THE *BEST* OF MEN.

A BARREL OF *APPLES* WAS LASHED ON DECK FOR *ANYONE* TO HELP HIMSELF THAT HAD A FANCY.

ONE DAY, JUST AFTER *SUNDOWN*, IT OCCURRED TO ME THAT I SHOULD LIKE AN APPLE.

I GOT BODILY INTO THE APPLE BARREL...AND FOUND THERE WERE *NONE* LEFT.

BUT, BEFORE I COULD *LEAVE*...

THERE WAS SOME THAT WAS *FEARED* OF PEW, AND SOME THAT WAS FEARED OF FLINT.

BUT FLINT HIS OWN SELF WAS FEARED OF *ME*, LONG JOHN SILVER.

I'VE HAD A'MOST *ENOUGH* O' CAP'N SMOLLETT. I WANT THEIR PICKLES AND *WINE!*

ISRAEL, YOU'LL *SPEAK SOFT* TILL I GIVE THE *WORD!*

THEN, DOOTY IS *DOOTY*, MATES. I GIVE MY VOTE: *DEATH*.

JOHN, YOU'RE A *MAN!*

LET'S HAVE A GO OF THE *RUM*.

YOU MAY FANCY THE *TERROR* I WAS IN*!*

THEN A SORT OF *BRIGHTNESS* FELL UPON ME IN THE BARREL. THE *MOON* HAD RISEN.

AND, THE *VOICE* OF THE *LOOKOUT* SHOUTED:

LAND HO!

THERE WAS A GREAT *RUSH* OF FEET ACROSS THE *DECK.*

SLIPPING IN AN INSTANT OUTSIDE MY *BARREL,* I DIVED BEHIND THE FORE-SAIL AND MADE A DOUBLE TOWARDS THE *STERN.*

I CAME OUT UPON THE OPEN DECK IN TIME TO JOIN *DR. LIVESEY* IN THE RUSH FOR THE

DR. *LIVESEY* CALLED ME TO HIS SIDE. AS SOON AS I WAS NEAR ENOUGH TO *SPEAK* AND NOT BE *OVERHEARD,* I SAID...

DOCTOR, GET THE CAPTAIN AND SQUIRE DOWN TO THE *CABIN,* AND THEN MAKE SOME *PRETENSE* TO SEND FOR ME.

I HAVE *TERRIBLE NEWS.*

I DID AND, AS *SHORT* AS I COULD MAKE IT, TOLD THE WHOLE *DETAILS* OF SILVER'S CONVERSATION.

NOW, HAWKINS, *SPEAK UP.*

CAPTAIN, YOU WERE RIGHT, AND I WAS *WRONG*. I AWAIT YOUR *ORDERS*.

WE MUST *GO ON.* IF I GAVE THE WORD TO GO ABOUT, THEY WOULD *RISE* AT ONCE. THE *BEST* THAT I CAN SAY IS *NOT MUCH.*

WE MUST KEEP A *BRIGHT LOOK-OUT* UNTIL WE KNOW WHO IN THE CREW WE CAN *TRUST*.

JIM CAN *HELP* US MORE THAN ANYONE. THE MEN ARE NOT *SHY* WITH HIM.

WE BROUGHT UP WITH *TREASURE ISLAND* ON ONE SIDE, AND *SKELETON ISLAND* ON THE OTHER.

MUTINY, IT WAS PLAIN, HUNG OVER US LIKE A THUNDER-CLOUD.

AND NOT ONLY WE PERCEIVED THE *DANGER.*

SILVER IS ANXIOUS TO TALK THEM *OUT* OF IT. I PROPOSE TO GIVE HIM THE *CHANCE.*

MY LADS! WE ARE ALL *TIRED* AND OUT OF SORTS.

A TURN ASHORE'LL HURT NOBODY. YOU CAN TAKE THE *GIGS*, AND AS MANY AS PLEASE CAN GO ASHORE FOR THE *AFTERNOON*.

I'LL FIRE A GUN HALF AN HOUR BEFORE *SUNDOWN*.

THE CREW ALL CAME OUT OF THEIR *SULKS* IN A MOMENT, AND GAVE A *CHEER* THAT STARTED THE ECHO IN A FAR-AWAY HILLL.

THE CAPTAIN LEFT SILVER TO *ARRANGE* THE PARTY. *SIX FELLOWS* WERE TO STAY ON BOARD, AND THE REMAINING *THIRTEEN*, INCLUDING SILVER, BEGAN TO *EMBARK*.

IT WAS THEN THAT IT CAME INTO MY HEAD THE FIRST OF THE *MAD NOTIONS* THAT CONTRIBUTED SO MUCH TO *SAVE* OUR LIVES.

IT WAS *PLAIN* THAT THE CABIN PARTY HAD NO PRESENT *NEED* OF MY ASSISTANCE. IT OCCURRED TO ME AT ONCE TO GO *ASHORE.*

IN A JIFFY I HAD SLIPPED OVER THE *SIDE,* AND CURLED UP IN THE FORESHEETS OF THE *NEAREST BOAT* ALMOST AT THE SAME MOMENT SHE *SHOVED OFF.*

IS THAT YOU, JIM? KEEP YOUR HEAD *DOWN.*

THE CREWS *RACED* FOR THE BEACH.

THE BOAT I WAS IN SHOT FAR *AHEAD.*

I CAUGHT A *BRANCH* AND SWUNG MYSELF OUT, AND PLUNGED INTO THE NEAREST *THICKET* WHILE SILVER AND THE REST WERE *BEHIND.*

JIM!
JIM!

I PAID NO HEED.

I *RAN* STRAIGHT BEFORE MY NOSE, TILL I COULD RUN *NO LONGER.*

SOON I HEARD THE LOW TONES OF A *HUMAN VOICE.*

I CRAWLED *UNDER COVER* OF THE NEAREST LIVE-OAK, AND SQUATTED THERE, HEARKENING, AS *SILENT* AS A MOUSE.

PRESENTLY I BEGN TO FEEL THAT I WAS *NEGLECTING* MY BUSINESS; THAT SINCE I HAD COME ASHORE, THE LEAST I COULD DO WAS TO *OVERHEAR* THEM.

CRAWLING ON ALL FOURS, I MADE *SLOWLY* TOWARDS THEM WHERE I COULD SEE *LONG JOHN SILVER* AND...

YOU'VE *KILLED* ALAN, HAVE YOU? KILL ME, TOO, IF YOU CAN. BUT I *DEFIES* YOU.

I BEGAN TO *EXTRICATE* MYSELF AND CRAWL BACK AGAIN, WITH WHAT *SPEED* AND *SILENCE* I COULD MANAGE.

AS I DID SO, I COULD HEAR *HAILS* COMING AND GOING BETWEEN THE *OLD BUCCANEER* AND HIS COMRADES, AND THIS SOUND OF *DANGER* LENT ME WINGS.

IT WAS ALL *OVER*, I THOUGHT. GOODBY TO THE *HISPANIOLA;* GOODBYE TO THE SQUIRE, THE DOCTOR, AND THE CAPTAIN*!*

THERE WAS *NOTHING* LEFT FOR ME BUT *DEATH* BY STARVATION, OR DEATH BY THE HANDS OF THE *MUTINEERS.*

AND THEN A *FRESH ALARM* BROUGHT ME TO A *STANDSTILL* WITH A THUMPING HEART.

MEANWHILE, ON THE *HISPANIOLA*...

MR. HANDS.

HERE ARE TWO OF US WITH A BRACE OF *PISTOLS* EACH. IF ANY ONE OF YOU SIX MAKE A *SIGNAL* OF ANY DESCRIPTION WHILE WE SEND *SUPPLIES* ASHORE...

...THAT MAN'S *DEAD.*

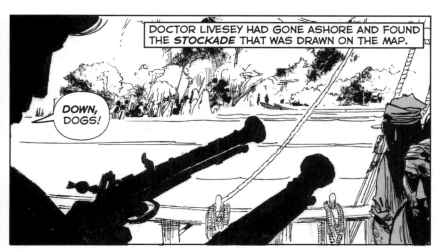

DOCTOR LIVESEY HAD GONE ASHORE AND FOUND THE *STOCKADE* THAT WAS DRAWN ON THE MAP.

DOWN, DOGS!

NOW HE, CAPTAIN SMOLLETT, THE SQUIRE, AND THOSE LOYAL, WERE *ABANDONING* SHIP...

...AND TAKING AS MUCH AS THEY COULD WITH THEM. WHAT THEY COULD *NOT TAKE,* PARTICULARLY THE GUNS, AMMUNTION, AND GUNPOWDER, THEY THREW *OVERBOARD.*

WHO ARE YOU?

BEN GUNN, I AM; AND I HAVEN'T SPOKE WITH A CHRISTIAN THESE THREE YEARS.

THREE YEARS! WERE YOU SHIPWRECKED?

NAY, MATE, MAROONED.

NOW YOU, WHAT DO YOU CALL YOURSELF, MATE?

JIM.

JIM... JIM.

AH, JIM, YOU'LL BLESS YOUR STARS, YOU WILL, YOU WAS THE FIRST THAT FOUND ME!

I WERE IN FLINT'S SHIP WHEN HE BURIED THE TREASURE. BILLY BONES WAS THE MATE. LONG JOHN, HE WAS THE QUARTERMASTER.

I WAS IN *ANOTHER SHIP* THREE YEARS BACK, AND WE *SIGHTED* THIS ISLAND.

"BOYS," I SAID, "HERE'S *FLINT'S TREASURE;* LET'S LAND AND FIND IT."

THE CAP'N WAS *DISPLEASED;* BUT MY MESSMATES WERE ALL OF A MIND, AND *LANDED.*

TWELVE DAYS THEY LOOKED FOR IT, AND EVERY DAY THEY HAD THE *WORSE WORD* FOR ME UNTIL ONE FINE MORNING *ALL HANDS* WENT ABOARD.

"AS FOR *YOU,* BENJAMIN GUNN. YOU CAN *STAY HERE,* AND FIND FLINT'S MONEY FOR YOURSELF," THEY SAYS.

K-BOOM K-BOOM

THEY HAVE BEGUN TO *FIGHT!* FOLLOW ME!

73

ONLY *ONE* OF THE GIGS IS BEING *MANNED*, CAPTAIN.

THE *CREW* OF THE OTHER IS GOING ROUND BY SHORE TO *CUT US OFF.*

IT'S NOT *THEM* I MIND. IT'S THE *ROUNDSHOT.*

CARPET BOWLS! MY LADY'S MAID COULDN'T *MISS* MAKING A HIT!

K-BOOM

SP-WSSH

HUNTER RUSHED FROM THE *STOCKADE* TO HELP THEM.

MAKE YOUR *BEST SPEED!*

THE **VOICES** OF THE BUCCANEERS RANG NEARER, AS DID THE **SOUNDS** OF THEIR FOOTFALLS AS THEY RAN.

THEN, AT THE **EDGE** OF THE WOOD AND NEAR THE **STOCKADE**...

UNH!

K-POW

K-POW

K-BAM

TOM!

DON'T YOU *TAKE ON*, SQUIRE. ALL'S *WELL* WITH TOM.

NO *FEAR* FOR A HAND THAT'S BEEN SHOT DOWN IN HIS *DUTY* TO CAPTAIN AND OWNER.

IT MAYN'T BE *GOOD DIVINITY,* BUT IT'S A FACT.

IT'S A PITY, SIR, WE LOST THAT *LOAD* ON THE BOAT. AS FOR *POWDER* AND SHOT, WE'LL DO.

BUT THE RATIONS ARE SHORT, VERY SHORT.

OHO! *BLAZE AWAY!*

YOU'VE LITTLE ENOUGH *POWDER* ALREADY, MY LADS.

CAPTAIN, THE HOUSE IS QUITE *INVISIBLE* FROM THE SHIP. IT WOULD BE THE *FLAG* THEY ARE *AIMING* AT. WOULD IT NOT BE WISER...

STRIKE MY COLORS! *NO, SIR,* NOT I!

DOCTOR! SQUIRE! CAPTAIN! HUNTER!

SOMEBODY *HAILING* US.

IT'S *JIM!*

I TOLD A LITTLE OF MY MEETING WITH *BEN GUNN*.

IS THIS *BEN GUNN* A MAN?

I DO NOT *KNOW*, SIR. I AM NOT VERY SURE WHETHER HE'S *SANE*.

A MAN WHO HAS BEEN THREE YEARS ON A *DESERT ISLAND*, JIM, CAN'T EXPECT TO *APPEAR* AS SANE AS YOU OR ME.

BEFORE SUPPER WAS EATEN WE BURIED OLD TOM IN THE SAND, AND STOOD ROUND HIM FOR A WHILE BARE-HEADED IN THE BREEZE.

HERE IT IS, CAP'N SMOLLETT. GIVE US THE *CHART* TO GET THE *TREASURE.* AND WE'LL OFFER YOU A *CHOICE.*

WE'LL CLAP YOU SOMEWHERE SAFE ASHORE. OR, WE'LL LEAVE YOU STORES *HERE* AND TELL THE *FIRST SHIP* I SIGHT TO PICK YOU UP

REFUSE THAT, AND YOU'VE SEEN THE LAST O ME BUT *MUSKET-BALLS.*

NOW YOU'LL *HEAR* ME. I'LL PUT A *BULLET* IIN YOUR BACK WHEN NEXT I *MEET* YOU.

GIVE ME A HAND *UP!*

LAUGH, BY THUNDER, *LAUGH!*

"BEFORE AN *HOUR'S* OUT...

...YE'LL LAUGH UPON THE OTHER SIDE."

WE'VE SOME TIME BEFORE THEY *ATTACK*, JIM. TELL ME ABOUT THIS *MAN* YOU MET IN THE WOODS.

HIS NAME IS *BEN GUNN* AND HE WAS A SIGHT TO BEHOLD. MR. GUNN WAS ABOARD *FLINT'S SHIP* WHEN FIRST HE CAME HERE. BILLY BONES WAS THE *MATE* AND SILVER THE QUARTERMASTER.

"FLINT WENT ASHORE FOR A WEEK WITH SIX MEN AND THE *TREASURE*.

"WHEN HE CAME BACK HE WAS *ALONE*. ALL SIX OF THE MEN WERE *DEAD* AND BURIED. HOW HE DID IT NO ONE KNEW."

"WHEN THEY ASKED ABOUT THE *TREASURE,* HE TOLD THEM THEY WERE FREE TO GO ASHORE...

"...BUT THE SHIP WAS OFF FOR MORE *PLUNDERING.*

"BEN GUNN LATER WAS ON *ANOTHER SHIP* THAT CAME ACROSS THIS ISLAND.

"HE CONVINCED THE *CREW* TO GO ASHORE TO FIND THE TREASURE. WHEN THEY DIDN'T, THEY *LEFT* HIM BEHIND.

"HE IS VERY *CONCERNED* ABOUT THE FACT THAT *SILVER* AND HIS MEN ARE ON THE ISLAND.

"HE WANTS TO MEET WITH *YOU* AND MAKE A *SQUARE DEAL.*"

"WHEN WE *PARTED,* HE ASKED ME TO GIVE THIS *MESSAGE* TO YOU:

"MEET HIM *TODAY* ABOUT NOON TO SIX BELLS.

"HE CLAIMED THAT HE WAS *RICH* AND WOULD *SHARE* WITH ME AND YOU TOO, IF ONLY FOR A *PASSAGE* OFF THE ISLAND.

"HE HAS SOMETHING TO *PROPOSE.*"

WAIT, JIM! CAPTAIN, I *HEAR* SOMETHING!

STEADY, MEN...

ROUND THE HOUSE, LADS! *ROUND* THE HOUSE!

MECHANICALLY I *OBEYED.*

NEXT *MOMENT* I WAS FACE TO FACE WITH ANDERSON.

I HAD NOT TIME TO BE *AFRAID.*

THUNK

THE *MUTINEERS* HAD BEEN READY TO MAKE AN END OF US. AND YET, IN A SHORT BREATH OF *TIME...*

...THE FIGHT WAS *OVER.*

THE *VICTORY* WAS OURS.

THE CAPTAIN'S *WOUNDED.*

HAVE THEY RUN?

ALL THAT *COULD.* BUT FIVE WILL NEVER RUN AGAIN.

THE CAPTAIN'S *WOUNDS* WERE GRIEVOUS, BUT NOT *DANGEROUS.* HE WAS SURE TO *RECOVER,* THE DOCTOR SAID.

AFTER DINNER, THE *DOCTOR* TOOK UP HIS HAT AND PISTOLS...

...CROSSED THE *PALISADE* ON THE NORTH SIDE, AND SET OFF BRISKLY THROUGH THE *TREES.*

IS DR. LIVESEY *MAD?*

WHY, *NO.* HE'S GOING NOW TO SEE *BEN GUNN.*

WITH SO MUCH *BLOOD* ABOUT ME, I TOOK A *DISGUST* OF THE PLACE THAT WAS ALMOST AS STRONG AS *FEAR.*

I WAS A *FOOL*, IF YOU LIKE, AND CERTAINLY I WAS GOING TO DO A FOOLISH, *OVER-BOLD ACT.*

BUT I WAS *DETERMINED* TO DO IT WITH ALL THE PRECAUTIONS IN MY POWER.

I DROPPED INTO THE HOLLOW, AND THERE, AS HE HAD TOLD ME, WAS *BEN GUNN'S BOAT,* HOME-MADE IF EVER ANYTHING WAS HOME-MADE.

MY *NOTION* WAS TO SLIP OUT UNDER COVER OF THE NIGHT, CUT THE *HISPANIOLA ADRIFT,* AND LET HER GO ASHORE WHERE SHE FANCIED.

DOWN I SAT TO WAIT FOR *DARKNESS.*

THERE WERE BUT *TWO POINTS* VISIBLE ON THE WHOLE ANCHORAGE.

ONE WAS THE GREAT *FIRE* ON SHORE, BY WHICH THE PIRATES LAY CAROUSING.

THE OTHER, THE *ANCHORED SHIP.*

ONE *CUT* WITH MY SEA-GULLY, AND THE *HISPANIOLA* WOULD GO HUMMING DOWN THE *TIDE.*

I HEARD THE SOUND OF *LOUD VOICES* FROM THE CABIN.

I WAS THINKING HOW BUSY DRINK AND THE DEVIL WERE IN THE CABIN OF THE HISPANIOLA, WHEN I WAS SURPRISED BY A SUDDEN LURCH OF THE CORACLE.

ALL AROUND ME WERE LITTLE *RIPPLES.*

BEHIND ME WAS THE *GLOW* OF THE CAMP FIRE.

THE CORACLE HEADED FOR THE *OPEN SEA.*

I DEVOUTLY RECOMMENDED MY *SPIRIT* TO ITS MAKER.

I THOUGHT I MUST FALL INTO SOME BARRAGING BREAKERS, WHERE ALL MY TROUBLES WOULD BE ENDED SPEEDILY.

THOUGH I COULD, PERHAPS, BEAR TO *DIE*, I COULD NOT BEAR TO *LOOK* UPON BY FATE AS IT APPROACHED. I LAY DOWN.

SLEEP AT LAST SUPERVENED, AND IN MY SEA-TOSSED CORACLE, I *DREAMED* OF HOME AND THE OLD ADMIRAL BENBOW.

IT WAS BROAD *DAY* WHEN I AWOKE, AND FOUND MYSELF TOSSING AT THE SOUTHWEST END OF *TREASURE ISLAND.*

I WAS *SURPRISED* HOW EASILY AND *SECURELY* MY LITTLE BOAT COULD RIDE.

EVERY NOW AND AGAIN I GAVE A *WEAK STROKE* OR TWO TO TURN THE CORACLE TO SHORE.

THEN I BEHELD A *SIGHT* THAT CHANGED THE NATURE OF MY THOUGHTS.

THE *HISPANIOLA!*

TO AND FRO, THE *HISPANIOLA* *SAILED* BY SWOOPS AND DASHES. IT BECAME PLAIN TO ME THAT NOBODY WAS *STEERING*.

I SPRANG TO MY FEET AND *LEAPED*.

NOT A *SOUL* WAS TO BE SEEN.

THEN, THE *MAIN BOOM* SWUNG INBOARD, AND SHOWED ME THE LEE AFTER-DECK.

THERE WAS *RED-CAP* AND ISRAEL HANDS. I FELT SURE THAT THEY HAD *KILLED* EACH OTHER IN THEIR DRUNKEN WRATH

...BRANDY...

MISTER *HANDS?*

AYE...! THAT SWAB, HE'S GOOD AND *DEAD* HE IS. HE WARN'T NO SEAMAN, ANYHOW.

AND WHERE MOUGHT *YOU* HAVE COME FROM?

WE STRUCK OUR *BARGAIN* ON THE SPOT. IN THREE MINUTES I HAD THE *HISPANIOLA* SAILIING EASILY BEFORE THE WIND ALONG THE *COAST* OF TREASURE ISLAND.

I WAS GREATLY ELATED WITH *MY NEW COMMAND*, AND PLEASED WITH THE BRIGHT, SUNSHINY WEATHER AND THESE DIFFERENT PROSPECTS OF THE COAST.

WITH NO *ANCHOR*, WE NEEDED TO HAVE THE SCHOONER *STRANDED* SAFE IN A *SHELTERED PLACE* SO THAT WHEN THE TIME CAME SHE COULD BE GOT OFF AGAIN.

THE SHORES OF THE *NORTH INLET* HAD AN ANCHORAGE THAT WAS *CALM*.

WE'RE NEAR THE BIT, CAP'N JIM! *NOW,* MY HEARTY!

I PUT THE HELM HARD UP, AND THE *HISPANIOLA SWUNG ROUND* RAPIDLY AND RAN STEM ON FOR THE LOW WOODED SHORE.

KRNCH

NOW, CAP'N...

AAAAAARRR!

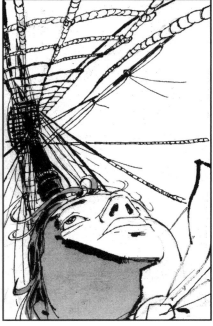

I WADED ASHORE IN *GREAT SPIRITS*. I HAD NOTHING NEARER MY FANCY THAN TO GET HOME TO THE *STOCKADE* AND BOAST OF MY *ACHIEVEMENTS*.

SO THINKING, I BEGAN TO SET MY FACE FOR THE *BLOCK-HOUSE*.

AT LAST I *ARRIVED*.

THERE WAS NOT A *SOUL* STIRRING.

I WALKED IN AND...

PIECES OF EIGHT!

PIECES OF EIGHT!

PIECES OF EIGHT!

SO, HERE'S *JIM HAWKINS*, SHIVER MY TIMBERS!

DROPPED IN LIKE, EH? WELL, *COME*, I TAKE THAT FRIENDLY.

I'VE ALWAYS LIKED YOU, I HAVE, FOR A LAD OF *SPIRIT*.

THE DOCTOR HIMSELF IS GONE DEAD AGAINST YOU. *"UNGRATEFUL SCAMP"* WAS WHAT HE SAID.

THE SHORT AND LONG IS: YOU CAN'T GO *BACK* TO YOUR OWN LOT.

THEY WON'T HAVE YOU.

I NEVER SEEN GOOD COME OUT O' *THREATENING*. IF YOU LIKE THE SERVICE, WELL, YOU'LL JOIN.

AND IF YOU DON'T, JIM, WHY YOU'RE *FREE* TO ANSWER *NO.*

TAKE YOUR *BEARINGS.* NONE OF US WON'T *HURRY* YOU, MATE.

119

THE NEXT MORNING.

BLOCK-HOUSE AHOY! HERE'S THE *DOCTOR*.

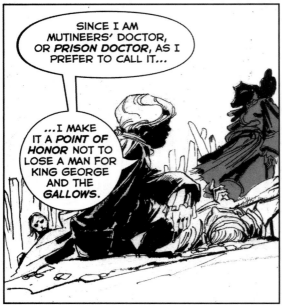

SINCE I AM MUTINEERS' DOCTOR, OR *PRISON DOCTOR*, AS I PREFER TO CALL IT...

...I MAKE IT A *POINT OF HONOR* NOT TO LOSE A MAN FOR KING GEORGE AND THE *GALLOWS*.

AND, WHEN HE WAS *DONE*, HE SAID...

YOU HAVE JIM. I SHOULD WISH TO HAVE A TALK WITH HIM.

HAWKINS, WILL YOU GIVE ME YOUR *WORD OF HONOR* AS A YOUNG GENTLEMAN NOT TO SLIP YOUR CABLE?

120

I READILY GAVE THE *PLEDGE* REQUIRED.

SO JIM, HERE YOU ARE. AS YOU HAVE BREWED SO YOU SHALL DRINK, MY BOY.

DOCTOR, YOU MIGHT SPARE ME. I HAVE *BLAMED* MYSELF ENOUGH. I SHOULD HAVE BEEN *DEAD* BY NOW, IF SILVER HADN'T STOOD FOR ME. WHAT I FEAR IS *TORTURE*. IF THEY TORTURE ME...

JIM. JIM, I CAN'T HAVE THIS. WHIP OVER, AND WE'LL *RUN* FOR IT.

SILVER TRUSTED ME. I PASSED MY WORD, AND *BACK* I GO.

BUT, DOCTOR, I GOT THE SHIP, PART BY LUCK AND PART BY RISKIING. SHE LIES IN NORTH INLET.

THE SHIP!

THERE IS A KIND OF *FATE* IN THIS.

SILVER! A PIECE OF ADVICE.

THE TREASURE. LOOK OUT FOR *SQUALLS* WHEN YOU FIND IT.

RAPIDLY I DESCRIBED TO HIM MY *ADVENTURES*. THEN...

AFTER BREAKFAST, WE LEFT TO FIND THE TREASURE. I WAS HORRIBLY *CAST DOWN*.

I HAD A LINE ABOUT MY *WAIST*. FOR ALL THE WORLD, I WAS LED LIKE A *DANCING BEAR*.

MIRY GROUND AND A MATTED, MARISH *VEGETATION*, GREATLY DELAYED OUR PROGRESS.

THE PARTY SPREAD IN A *FAN SHAPE*.

SILVER AND I FOLLOWED.

FROM TIME TO TIME, I HAD TO LEND HIM A *HAND*, OR HE WOULD HAVE MISSED HIS *FOOTING*.

WE HAD PROCEEDED FOR ABOUT HALF A MILE WHEN...

AHHHH!

HE CAN'T HAVE FOUND THE TREASURE!

THAT'S *CLEAN* A-TOP!

OTHERS BEGAN TO *RUN* IN THE DIRECTION OF THE CRY.

WE FOLLOWED.

WHAT WE *FOUND*...

...WAS SOMETHING VERY *DIFFERENT*.

A *HUMAN SKELETON.* I BELIEVE A CHILL STRUCK FOR A MOMENT TO EVERY HEART.

TAKE A *BEARING* ALONG THE LINES OF THEM BONES.

IT WAS DONE. THE COMPASS READ *EAST/SOUTH-EAST AND BY EAST*.

THOUGHT SO. THIS WAS FLINT'S DOING YOU CAN BE SURE. THIS IS ONE OF THE SIX HE KILLED. THIS ONE HE HAULED HERE TO BE A COMPASS.

THEY'RE *LONG BONES*, AND THE HAIR'S BEEN YELLOW. THAT WOULD BE *ALLARDYCE*. YOU MIND ALLARDYCE, TOM MORGAN?

AYE, I MIND HIM. HE OWED ME MONEY AND TOOK MY *KNIFE* ASHORE WITH HIM.

128

COME, COME, *STOW* THIS TALK. HE'S *DEAD* AND HE DON'T WALK, THAT I KNOW.

FETCH AHEAD FOR THE *DOUBLOONS*.

COME, THIS WON'T DO! STAND BY TO *COME ABOUT.* THAT'S SOMEONE SKYLARKING...

...SOMEONE THAT'S *FLESH AND BLOOD,* AND YOU MAY LAY TO THAT.

DARBY M'GRAW! DARBY M'GRAW!

FETCH AFT THE RUM, DARBY!

THAT FIXES IT! LET'S GO!

THEY WAS HIS *LAST WORDS!* HIS LAST WORDS ABOVE BOARD.

SHIPMATES, I'LL NOT BE *BEAT* BY MAN OR *DEVIL.*

I NEVER WAS FEARED OF FLINT IN HIS *LIFE* AND I'LL FACE HIM *DEAD!*

BELAY THERE, JOHN! DON'T YOU *CROSS* A SPERRIT!

IT WAS EXTRAORDINARY HOW THEIR *SPIRITS* HAD RETURNED.

NOT LONG AFTER, HEARING NO FURTHER *SOUND,* THEY SHOULDERED THE TOOLS AND SET FORTH AGAIN.

WE SOON FOUND THE NEXT MARKER, A *TALL TREE.*

IT WAS HARD FOR ME TO KEEP UP WITH THE *RAPID PACE* OF THE TREASURE-HUNTERS.

HUZZA, MATES, ALL TOGETHER!

THE FOREMOST BROKE INTO A *RUN*.

SUDDENLY NOT TEN YARDS FURTHER, WE BEHELD THEM *STOP*.

A LOW *CRY* AROSE.

BEFORE US WAS A GREAT *EXCAVATION*, NOT VERY RECENT.

ON ONE OF THE BOARDS I SAW THE NAME *WALRUS*, THE NAME OF FLINT'S *SHIP*.

THE CACHE HAD BEEN FOUND. THE TREASURE WAS *GONE!*

JIM, TAKE *THAT*.

AND STAND BY FOR *TROUBLE*.

BAM

GEORGE, I RECKON I *SETTLED* YOU.

FORWARD! DOUBLE QUICK, MY LADS.

AND SO IT'S *YOU,* BEN GUNN. WELL, YOU'RE A *NICE ONE* TO BE SURE.

BEN, BEN, TO THINK AS YOU'VE *DONE* ME!

HOW DO, *MISTER SILVER?*

AS WE *PROCEEDED* TO THE BOATS, THE DOCTOR RELATED WHAT HAD TAKEN PLACE.

BEN GUNN WAS THE *HERO* FROM BEGINNING TO END. HE HAD *FOUND* THE TREASURE. *DUG* IT UP. AND *CARRIED* IT AWAY.

THE DOCTOR HAD **WORMED** THIS SECRET FROM HIM.

WHEN HE SAW THE **ANCHORAGE** DESERTED, HE WENT TO SILVER.

HE GAVE HIM THE CHART, WHICH WAS NOW **USELESS**.

AND THE SHIP'S **STORES**.

BEN GUNN'S CAVE WAS WELL SUPPLIED WITH **GOAT'S MEAT** SALTED BY HIMSELF.

FINDING OUT THAT JIM WAS TO BE AMONG THE PIRATES AS THEY MADE THEIR DISAPPOINTING **DISCOVERY**, THE DOCTOR, BEN GUNN, AND GRAY HURRIED TO THE TREE.

TO *SLOW* THEM DOWN, BEN GUNN WORKED UPON THE *SUPERSTITIONS* OF HIS FORMER SHIPMATES.

BY THE TIME HE WAS *FINISHED,* WE REACHED SQUIRE TRELAWNEY AND BEN GUNN'S *CAVE.*

JOHN SILVER, YOU'RE A PRODIGIOUS VILLAIN AND *IMPOSTOR!* I AM TOLD NOT TO PROSECUTE YOU. WELL, I WILL NOT.

THANK YOU KINDLY, SIR.

WE HAD A GREAT *SUPPER* THAT NIGHT IN BEN GUNN'S *CAVE,* SURROUNDED BY CAPTAIN FLINT'S *TREASURE.*

FOR SEVERAL DAYS WE LOADED THE **TREASURE** ON THE HISPANIOLA. THEN WE RAISED ANCHOR AND **LEFT** THE SURVIVING MUTINEERS. ONE SENT A **SHOT** THROUGH THE MAINSAIL.

WE WERE SO SHORT OF MEN THAT **EVERYONE** HAD TO BEAR A HAND. ONLY CAPTAIN SMOLLETT, STILL RECOVERING FROM HIS **WOUNDS**, WAS SPARED.

IT WAS JUST AT **SUNDOWN** WHEN WE CAST ANCHOR AT A MOST BEAUTIFUL LAND-LOCKED GULF.

THE DOCTOR, THE SQUIRE, AND I WENT TO VISIT THE *TOWN.* WHEN WE RETURNED, BEN GUNN WAS ON DECK *ALONE.*

HE MADE US A *CONFESSION.* SILVER WAS *GONE.* GUNN HAD HELPED HIS *ESCAPE,* ASSURING US HE HAD ONLY DONE SO TO *PRESERVE* OUR LIVES.

THE SEA COOK HAD NOT GONE EMPTY-HANDED. HE REMOVED ONE *SACK* OF COIN WORTH THREE OR FOUR HUNDRED *GUNEAS.*

I THINK WE WERE ALL *PLEASED* TO BE SO CHEAPLY *QUIT* OF LONG JOHN SILVER.

TO MAKE A LONG STORY SHORT, WE MADE A *GOOD CRUISE* HOME. ALL OF US HAD AN AMPLE *SHARE* OF THE TREASURE, AND USED IT WISELY OR *FOOLISHLY,* ACCORDING TO OUR NATURE.

OF SILVER WE HAVE HEARD *NO MORE.*

THAT FORMIDABLE *SEAFARING MAN* WITH ONE LEG HAS AT LAST *GONE* CLEAN OUT OF MY LIFE.

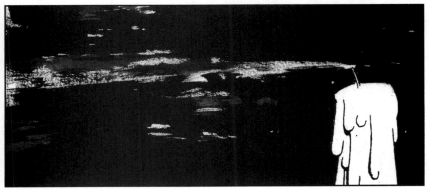